Yoga with My Foster Mom

Yoga with My Foster Mom

Zoevera A. Jackson

Table of Contents

Dedication

This book is dedicated to my two nieces Riann and Raquel. As you continue to learn and practice your yoga skills remember to make it your own. Be Bold. Embrace what makes you different, and share your yoga with the world.

Introduction

This story takes place in a galaxy of dreams that come true. It is the dream of two girls to learn yoga from their foster mom. The story is told through their eyes and in their own words. In the process, they also learn that their yoga poses do not have to be perfect or exactly like their foster mom to be correct. Instead, both girls learn to enjoy the practice of yoga by making it their own within their physical limits and abilities.

This book promotes being a foster parent and using yoga as a way to spend quality time with your foster child.

What is Yoga

Yoga is the practice of controlled movement and concentrated and controlled breathing.

Kids who practice yoga experience both physical and mental calming. Physically it enhances their flexibility, strength, coordination, and body aware-ness. In addition, their concentration and sense of calmness and relaxation improve.

Yoga teaches acceptance and tolerance of others. In practing yoga, kids learn early in life that all livng beings are to be cherished and respected as they are.

Key Words for Setting the Intent for Yoga Practice

Hope, Love, Faith, Patience, Resilence

Honor, Reserve, Gratitude, Compassion

My foster mom loves yoga.

She practices yoga every day!

My foster mom lays out all her yoga tools that she often uses.

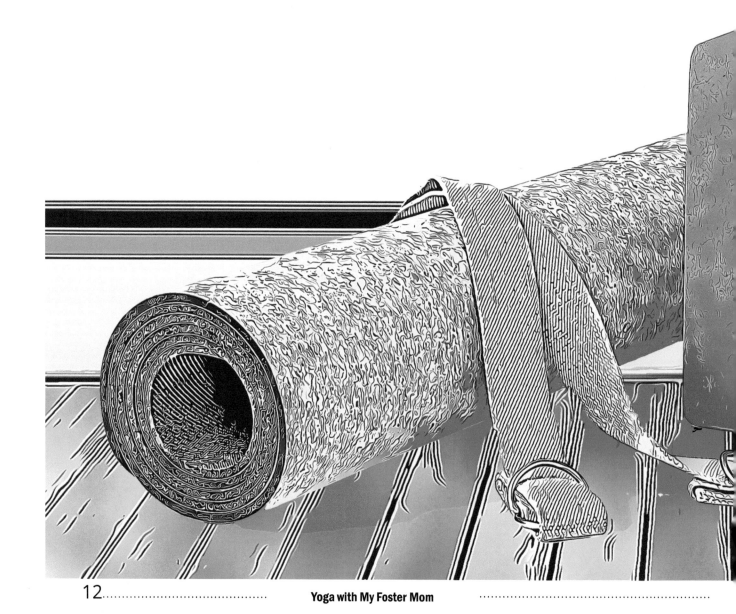

Yoga mat,

Yoga strap,

Yoga block.

My foster mom starts in a seated pose with praying hands.

She sets the intent for our yoga practice.

My foster mom teaches yoga classes to people all over the world.

Yoga with My Foster Mom

She tells them to just breath
and move   with ease
              and comfort.

My foster mom loves posing like a Tree.

Yoga with My Foster Mom

I love tree pose because it makes me feel strong, tall, and balanced.

My foster mom shows us the warrior one pose.

This pose makes us feel like we are rockets in flight to the moon.

Our foster mom shows balance and flexability in bow pose.

I love bow pose even if I look and feel different doing it.

Our foster mom makes us feel confident and strong.

Yoga with My Foster Mom

In hero pose we show our girl power.

We lay down on the floor in reclined twist.

We prepare to end our yoga practice calm and relaxed in savasana.

We love our foster mom because she shares her yoga practice with us.

She always ends her yoga practice in seated meditation pose.

Zoevera's Yoga

Prayer Pose

Tadasana

Modified Tree

Reverse Warrior

Poses Diagram

Triangle Pose

Boat Pose

Bow Pose

Cross Legged Meditation Pose

Raquel's Yoga

Hero Pose

Tree Pose

Warrior One

Poses Diagram

Reverse Warrior

Downward Facing Dog

Childs Pose

Riann's Yoga

Prayer Pose

Hero Pose

Bow Pose

Poses Diagram

Warrior One

Reverse Warrior

Savasana

COLOR ME

Raquel Hayes

8 years-old

Favorite yoga pose: Reverse Warrior

REVERSE

WARRIOR

COLOR ME

Riann Chandler

6 years-old

Favorite yoga pose: Hero Pose

About the Author

Zoevera Jackson is an entrepreneur, health coach, mentor, and public speaker. She became a foster parent because she wanted to go above and beyond helping children in need. She wanted to become actively engaged in helping to fight the problems of homelessness, mental health, substance abuse, domestic abuse, and poverty. As a foster parent, she not only became a care-taker but she became an instant role model for the biological parents.

Zoevera has served as a foster parent for the past three years with three different foster care agencies and has taken care of three different sets of siblings ranging in age from three to seventeen. Her experience as a foster parent has truly opened her heart and caused her to be more patient, loving, understanding, and perseverant. As a yoga teacher, she enjoys sharing her skill and passion for yoga and meditation with all of her foster children.

Contact Info

Email: info@zbodyllc.com

Website: www.zbodyllc.com

About the Illustrator

Janine Coogler-Hudson is the CEO of Mobi9Tech, a full service digital marketing agency. She is a talented entrepreneur dedicated to helping small businesses fulfill their visions.

Over the past three years, Janine created many websites, graphics and implemented various software to help small businesses enhance their productivity.

As a graphic designer, Janine was excited to work with Zoevera to produce quality illustrations for the yoga book. She hopes the vibrant colors and artistry help children visualize how yoga can create a bond between foster children and their foster parents.

Janine is a wife and mother of three children ranging in the ages of thirteen to sixteen. She also homeschools her daughter who is a Junior Olympic Gymnast.

Contact Info
Email: jhudson@mobi9tech.com

Website: www.mobi9tech.com

CPSIA information can be obtained
at www.ICGtesting.com
Printed in the USA
BVHW020105090321
602095BV00004B/25